To Alex for all the time we spent listening to clocks.
And to Billy and Todd for keeping me wound.
— Debbie

To my family for always supporting me.
— Sarah

Kane Miller, A Division of EDC Publishing

Text copyright © Debbie Bernstein LaCroix, 2011
Illustrations copyright © Sarah Chalek, 2011

Library of Congress Control Number: 2010941082

Manufactured by Regent Publishing Services, Hong Kong
Printed April 2011 in ShenZhen, Guangdong, China

1 2 3 4 5 6 7 8 9 10

ISBN: 978-1-935279-85-3

It's Almost Time

Written by Debbie Bernstein LaCroix
Illustrated by Sarah Chalek

Kane Miller
A DIVISION OF EDC PUBLISHING

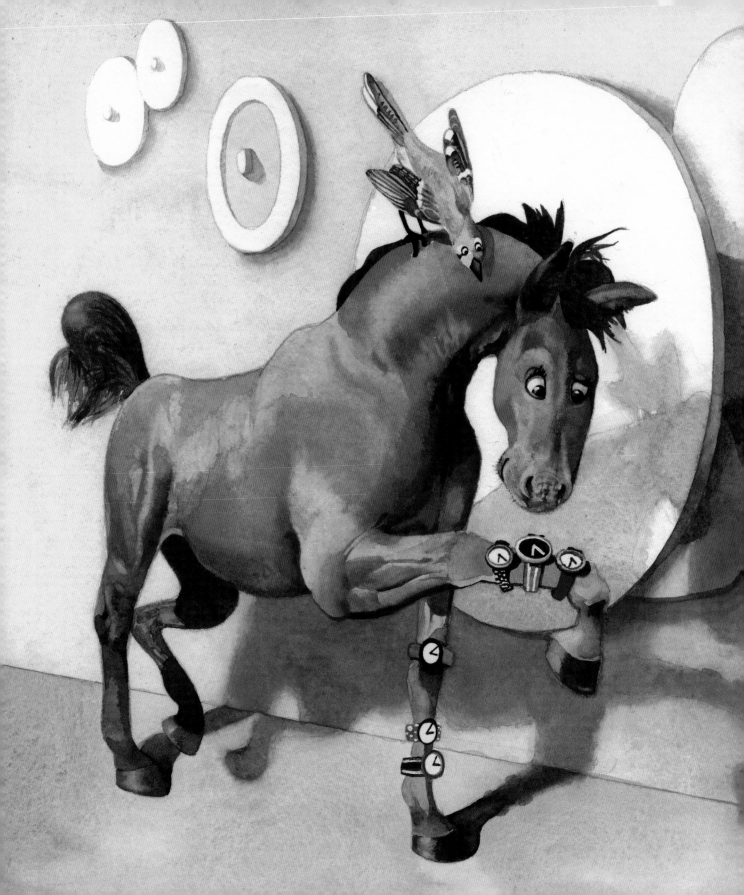

Tick-tick-tock.

It's almost time.

The gears are winding,
getting ready to chime.

Tick-tock, tick-tock, steady and true.

Tick-tock, tick-tock, one minute till *cuckoo.*

Thump, thump, thump, thump,
a giant clock ticks.

Tickety-tockety,
Tickety-tockety,
a smaller clock clicks.

Clunk, clunk, clunk, clunk,
go the hands of another.

Tick, tick, tick, tick,
all in time with each other.

The pendulum swings side to side,
to and from, waiting for that special
moment to come.

Sssssshhh, listen to what the clocks have to say.

Sssssshhh, listen as the seconds tick away…

10, 9, 8, 7, 6, 5, 4, 3, 2, 1

Mary had a little lamb,
plays the baby's clock softly.

Bum, bum, bum, bummmm, serenades the anniversary clock sweetly.

Beep, beep, beep, beep, babbles the alarm
clock annoyingly.

Bzzzzzzz, cries the buzzer clock angrily.

Cuckoo! Cuckoo! echos the little bird clock repeatedly.

Ding, ding, ding! Ding, ding, ding! gossips
the kitchen clock impatiently.

Clang, clang, hammers
the wall clock steadily.

Dinggg, donggg!
Dinggg, donggg!
dins the hall clock clearly.

Cock-a-dooodle-dooooo, crows the bedroom clock happily.

Bonggg! Bonggg! bellows the grandfather clock proudly.

Boooommm! Boooommm!
Booommm! Booommm!
clamors the tower clock loudly!

Little Lamb!

Bummmm!

BEEP!BEEP!

Bzzzzzzz!

CUCKOO!

DING!

CLANG!

Dinggg, donggg!

COCK-A-DOOODLE-DOOOOO!

BONGGG!

BOOOOMMM!

Then, silence.
Unless you listen closely...

Softly the clocks tick tock in time, just 59 minutes until they will chime.